D0323705

The Night Before Cat-mas

By
Virginia Unser

Illustrated by
Karen Anagnost

PETER PAUPER PRESS, INC.
WHITE PLAINS, NEW YORK

Designed by Arlene Greco
Illustrations copyright © 1998
Karen Anagnost

Text copyright © 1998
Peter Pauper Press, Inc.
202 Mamaroneck Avenue
White Plains, NY 10601
ISBN 0-88088-834-2
Printed in China
7 6 5 4 3 2 1

The Night Before Cat-mas

'Twas the night

before Cat-mas

When all through

the house

Not a kitten was stirring

Nor chasing a mouse.

The stockings were hung

By the chimney with care

In hopes that St. Kittyclaws

Soon would be there.

The kittens were nestled

All snug in their beds

While visions of catnip

Danced in their heads.

Ma Tab with her whiskers

And I in my cap

Had just settled down

For a winter's catnap.

When outside the house,

Came such noise

and such strife,

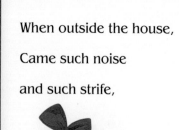

So startled was I

That I used up a life!

I jumped to the window

And gave a small "mew."

I perched in the moonlight,

Enjoying the view.

The sight of the snowdrifts

So cold and so white,

Made me purrfectly glad

To be indoors tonight!

When, what to my wondering

Eyes did appear,

But a feline-sized sleigh

And eight tiny cat-deer,

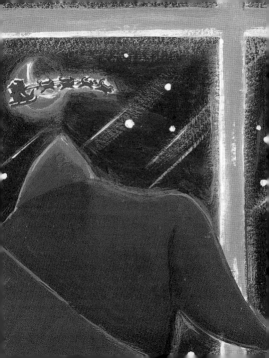

With a little old driver

So lively and fit,

I knew in a moment

He must be St. Kit.

So quickly they flew

And with such grace

they came!

Then Kittyclaws smiled

And mewed out

their names:

"Now Felix! Now Patches!

Now, Mittens and Muffy!

On, Twinkle! On, Whiskers!

On, Tiger and Fluffy!

"Don't wake up the collie!

Watch out for the wall!

Go on past the mailbox!

And try not to fall!"

As kittens will pounce

On a fat ball of string,

Tails all a-tumbling,

Ready to spring,

So up to the door frame

The felines all flew

With a sleigh full of toys

And St. Kittyclaws too.

And then in a twinkling

I heard by the door

The scratching and pawing

Of each little claw.

As I drew in my head

And was turning around,

Kittyclaws came

Through the door with a bound.

He was dressed all in fur

From his head to his feet

And his whiskers

were sprinkled

With flurries and sleet.

A bundle of toys

He had flung on his back

And he looked like a peddler

Just opening his pack.

His eyes—

how they twinkled!

His whiskers—

so merry!

His tail was

so fluffy,

His nose like

a cherry!

His droll little mouth

Was drawn up like a bow,

And the fur on his chin

Was as white as the snow;

The stump of a pipe

He held tight in his teeth,

And the smoke it encircled

His head like a wreath;

He had a broad face

And a round little belly

That shook when he purred

Like a bowl full of jelly.

He was chubby and plump,

A right jolly old cat,

And I laughed when I saw him

Looking like that;

A wink of his eye and

A flick of his tail:

I knew our stockings

Would bulge without fail;

He made not a sound;

He was silent and swift.

Each of the kittens

Was given a gift.

He washed his paws quickly,

And, twitching his nose,

He gave me a nod.

Up the chimney he rose.

He sprang to his sleigh,

And "meow"ed to the team.

They all flew away

In the moonlight's

soft gleam.

But I heard him meow

Ere he drove out of sight—

"Happy Cat-mas to all

and to all a Good Night!"